LONGM

Alice in Wonderland

Lewis Carroll

Simplified by D K Swan
Illustrations by Sir John Tenniel

Longman

Longman Group UK Limited,
Longman House, Burnt Mill, Harlow,
Essex CM20 2JE, England
and Associated Companies throughout the world.

This simplified edition © Longman Group UK Limited 1987

First published 1987
Eighth impression 1993

ISBN 0-582-52278-1

Set in 12/14 point Linotron 202 Versailles
Printed in Hong Kong
GC/08

Acknowledgements

Coloured Tenniel illustrations © 1980 Macmillan Publishers
Limited.

The cover background is a wallpaper design called NUAGE,
courtesy of Osborne and Little plc.

Stage 1: 500 word vocabulary

Please look under *New words* at the back of this book
for explanations of words outside this stage.

Contents

Introduction

Lewis Carroll

People did not expect Charles Lutwidge Dodgson to write nonsense. He was a well-known and respected teacher of mathematics at Oxford University from 1854 to 1881. Mathematics, the science of numbers, is a world of logic. In logic, you reason carefully, working from one certain fact to the next. There is no nonsense in logic or mathematics.

Perhaps that is why the respected mathematician didn't use his own name when, in 1865, he wrote a book of nonsense, a book which stands logic on its head. As the writer of *Alice in Wonderland*, Dodgson called himself Lewis Carroll.

Not that the nonsense in *Alice* is just foolish. We find it strange, but it seems to be not wholly unreasonable. It is dream logic instead of daylight logic, but it is logic – of a kind. That is partly why grown-up people enjoy it.

Alice sometimes wonders about the logic.

> "Does *your* watch tell you what year it is?"
>
> "No," Alice answered, "but that's

because it's the same year for a very long time."

"And *my* watch doesn't tell the time because it's always tea time."

Alice wondered about that, but she said nothing.

Sometimes she doesn't wonder. The reasoning seems all right.

"But I don't want to meet mad people," Alice said.

"Oh, there's no way *not* to meet them. We're all mad here. I'm mad. You're mad."

"How do you know I'm mad?" Alice asked.

"You must be mad," the Cat said. "Everybody who comes here is mad. Are you going to play croquet with the Queen today?"

"That would be very nice," said Alice, "but nobody has asked me yet."

But *Alice in Wonderland* was not written as a book for grown-ups. It was for children. In 1865 there were certainly other books that had been written for children and young people. Nearly all of them were written to teach, and most of all to teach the readers to be good and to behave well. There were very few books to make the young reader laugh, and very few books to take him or her into a world of imagination. *Alice in Wonder-*

land must have been a great surprise.

But are the things that happen in *Alice* really so surprising? We – children and grown-ups – have all been in Wonderland in our dreams. We are not really surprised when Alice changes her size; we have done that in our own dreams. The Cheshire Cat appears and disappears. Why not? The playing-card people are frightening one minute, and "only a pack of cards" the next minute. Of course. We all know the feeling.

We know the people. We all know at least one fussy man like the King of Hearts. We could name a person like the Queen of Hearts, who shouts and gives orders – but doesn't really do much harm. We know somebody rather like every one of the creatures in the book, and we needn't be surprised at the things they say and do.

But it was probably very surprising when people found out that "Lewis Carroll" was really the serious mathematics teacher Charles Dodgson.

Chapter 1
Down the rabbit hole

Alice and her big sister were sitting on the grass. Her sister was reading a book, but Alice had nothing to read. She looked at her sister's book again. There were no pictures in it.

"What good is a book without pictures?" she wondered.

It was a very hot day, and Alice wondered what to do. "I'm so sleepy," she said to herself. "Shall I look for some flowers, or is it too hot?"

She saw a leaf falling from a tree, but she was too sleepy to look at it.

Just then, a white rabbit ran by, very near to her. That does not happen every day, but Alice did not wonder about it. She did not wonder very much even when the rabbit said to itself, "Oh! Oh! I shall be too late!"

But she did wonder when the rabbit took a watch out of its pocket and looked at it.

"A rabbit with a pocket?" Alice asked herself. "And a watch in it?"

She jumped up and ran after the White Rabbit. She was just in time to see him go down a big rabbit hole.

Alice went into the hole too. She didn't stop to wonder how she could get out again.

The rabbit hole went along just under the

ground, and then ... Alice was falling ... down ... down ... down.

She was not falling quickly. She had time to wonder "What's going to happen next?" She looked down, but there was no light there.

Down, down, down. "Oh!" she said, "it's a long way. I shall never be afraid of falling again. I wonder where the hole will come out."

Down, down, down. "Will Dinah wonder where I am tonight?" Alice asked herself. (Dinah was Alice's cat.) "Will they remember her milk at tea time? Oh, Dinah! Why aren't you here with me? There are no mice here, but there may be some bats. Do cats eat bats, I wonder?" Alice was beginning to get sleepy. "Do cats eat bats?" she asked herself. "Do cats eat bats?" And sometimes she asked, "Do bats eat cats?"

THUMP! BUMP! Alice came down on something that was not very hard.

She sat up quickly. She could still see the White Rabbit, far away along the rabbit hole.

"Run!" Alice told herself, and she ran very quickly after the White Rabbit.

"Oh, my ears!" she heard him say. "How late it's getting!" Then he went quickly through an opening at the side of the rabbit hole.

Alice ran through the opening. She was in a long hall, and she could not see the White Rabbit.

There were doors on every side of the hall, but she could not open any of them, and she could not find the opening from the rabbit hole.

"What can I do?" she wondered. Then she saw a little table. It was a glass table, and there was a very small golden key on it. "Will it open one of the doors?" she wondered. She went to all the doors, but the key was much too small to open any of them. "It must open something," she told herself.

Then she saw a very little door, hidden near one of the big doors. The little key opened it. Alice put her head down and looked through it into a very beautiful garden. She could see a lot of flowers and grass, and she wanted to go there. But the door was much too small. Sadly she shut it again and took the key back to the table.

"Why can't I become smaller?" Alice wondered. "It's not like home here – it's more magic – so there must be a way to get smaller." She looked at the glass table. There was a little bottle on it. ("That was *not* on the table before," Alice told herself.) She read a note on the bottle. It was in very good, big writing: "DRINK ME".

"I shall try just a little," Alice said, "a very little." She tried it, and it was very nice. She drank some more.

"Oh! My feet are much smaller and much nearer," Alice said. "I must be very small now."

She was. "Now I can go through the little door," she told herself. She went to the door, but

3

Alice finds a little bottle on the table

she could not open it, and the key was on the glass table. She could see it through the glass, but she was now much too small to get it. She tried to get to it up one of the glass legs, but she could not.

The poor little girl sat down and cried.

"Alice! Alice!" she said bravely. "It's no good crying like that. Stop it at once!" She sometimes spoke to herself like that, but it did not help her this time. She was still crying when she saw a little glass box under the table.

Alice opened the box. There was a very small cake in it. "EAT ME", she read.

"Yes, I shall eat it," Alice said. "If I grow bigger after that, I can get the key. If I grow smaller, I can get under the door into the garden." So she ate the cake.

Chapter 2
The pool of tears

Alice grew bigger. "How quickly I'm growing!" she said. And then, "Oh!" she cried, as her head hit the ceiling.

"I must go into that garden," she thought. "This hall is too small for me now."

She took the little golden key and went quickly to the garden door. She was much too big to go through it.

Poor Alice! She sat down and began to cry again. Because she was so big, the tears that fell from her eyes were very big too. They made a big pool.

"Stop crying!" Alice told herself. "You're a big girl" (and she *was* big – very big) "and you mustn't cry." But she couldn't stop the big tears, and soon there was a pool of tears all round her.

After a time, she heard little feet running towards her, and then she saw the White Rabbit coming back. He had his best clothes on, and he had two very clean white gloves in one hand and a fan in his other hand.

"Oh, the Duchess, the Duchess!" Alice heard him saying. "How angry she'll be because I'm late!"

Alice wanted to ask him for help. She tried to speak in her nicest way as she said, "Please——"

The White Rabbit jumped. The word came from the ceiling, and he was afraid. He ran away as quickly as he could, and the gloves and the fan fell from his hands.

Alice took up the very small gloves and the fan. It was hot in the hall, so she began to fan herself with the fan.

"Am I changed?" she wondered. "I was myself yesterday, but things are not the same today. If I'm not me, who am I? I don't want to be my friend Mabel because she doesn't know very much. I know much more than she does." Alice stopped. "Do I know more?" she wondered. "I'll try. I'll try to say four times. Four times one is four. Four times two is eight. Four times three is nine. Four times four is... Oh!" She began to cry again.

They were only small tears. One of them fell on her hand, and she looked down. There was a glove on the other hand.

She had put one of the White Rabbit's little gloves on.

"How can I have done that?" she thought. "I must be growing small."

She stood up and walked to the table again. "I'll see how big I am," she said.

The table was a long way up. Alice was very small, and she was quickly becoming smaller. "The fan!" she thought. "The fan's making me smaller." She threw it down.

7

"I'm so small that I can go through the door," she thought, and she ran towards it. She had not run far when – SPLASH – she fell into a lot of water. "I have fallen into the sea," she thought.

It wasn't the sea. It was the pool of tears that she had made when she was very big.

"Why did I cry so much?" Alice said.

She heard something splashing about in the pool near her. "It must be a very big fish or sea animal," she thought. But then she remembered that she herself was very small, and she soon saw that it was a mouse that had fallen into the water.

"I wonder if it can speak," Alice thought. "This place is not the same as home, so I'll speak to it. Oh, Mouse!" she said. "Do you know the way out of this pool?"

There was no answer. "Is it a French mouse?" Alice wondered. She tried to remember some French words. The words that began her school French book were the words for: Where is my cat? So she said them: "Où est ma chatte?"

There was a great splashing, and the Mouse moved away as quickly as he could.

"Oh!" Alice cried. "Please don't be angry! I didn't remember that mice don't like cats."

"Don't like cats!" the Mouse said. (He was very angry.) "Would *you* like cats if you were me?"

8

"No," Alice said. "No. But I think you would like Dinah. She is a nice, dear thing." Alice was speaking mostly to herself. "She never makes a noise, and she's very good. She catches all the mice——Oh! You're angry again! We will not speak about Dinah any more——"

"We!" the Mouse cried. "I *never* speak about cats! I don't want to hear any more about them."

Alice quickly tried to speak about other things. "Perhaps ... " she said, "perhaps you like dogs?" The Mouse did not answer, so Alice began again: "There is a very nice little dog near our house. You would love it. It likes playing with children, but it works too. Its home is on a farm, and the farmer says that it helps him a lot. It kills all the m—— Oh!"

The Mouse was very angry. He splashed his way to the side of the pool and got out of the water. Alice went after him.

There were a lot of animals and birds which had fallen into the pool: a duck, and a dodo, and others with names that Alice did not know. They splashed after Alice and got out of the water.

Chapter 3
A Caucus race

Alice was very cold after being in the pool, and all the animals and birds were cold and unhappy.

Alice did not wonder about it when they began to speak to her.

"The best thing if you are cold," the Dodo said, "is to have a race – a Caucus race."

None of the other birds or animals said anything, but the Dodo was waiting for a question, so Alice asked, "What *is* a Caucus race?"

"I could tell you," the Dodo said, "but the best thing is to do it."

The Dodo made marks to show where to run. There was no place to begin running. There was no place to run to. There was no "One, two, three, *go*!" They began running when they liked, and they stopped when they liked. Only the Dodo knew when the race was over. When everybody was hot again and happy, the Dodo called out: "The race is over!"

Then they all stood round the Dodo and asked, "Who has won?"

The Dodo could not answer at once. He sat for a long time with a finger to his head, and at last he said: "Everybody has won. Everybody must have a prize."

"But who is to give the prizes?" the Mouse

and a lot of other animals asked.

"*She* is," the Dodo said, looking at Alice.

"Prizes! Prizes!" all the birds and animals cried, standing round Alice.

Alice was not ready for this, but she put her hand in her pocket. She found a small box of very small sweets in it. (It was a good thing that the water had not got into it.) There was just one sweet for each of the birds and animals.

"But she must have a prize herself, you know," the Mouse said.

"Yes," the Dodo answered. He told Alice to find another prize in her pocket.

"I only have the box," Alice said.

"Give it to me." The Dodo put his hand out, and Alice put the box into it.

They all stood round Alice again, and the Dodo gave her the box, saying: "Please take this very beautiful box with our thanks."

The next thing was to eat the sweets. There was some noise and crying about this. The sweets were too small for the big birds: they did not last. They were too big for the small birds. "Quick! Pat them on their backs!" Alice cried.

At last the sweets were all gone, and the birds and animals sat round in a ring and waited for something to happen.

"If Dinah were here, I should be very happy," Alice said. She said it to herself, but her new

Alice with the Dodo

friends heard the words.

"And who is Dinah, may I ask?" the Dodo said.

Alice was always ready to speak about her friend the cat.

"Dinah's our cat. She's very nice. And she's very quick. You should see her catching mice. She's very good at catching birds too— Oh, why have they all gone?"

All the animals and birds had gone. Alice was alone again. "They don't like me to speak about Dinah," she told herself. "Nobody likes Dinah down here, but she's the best cat of all. I wonder if I shall ever see her again."

Alice began to cry again because she was alone, but she heard little feet coming towards her, and she stopped crying. "Perhaps it's the Mouse," she thought.

Chapter 4
The White Rabbit's house

It was not the Mouse. It was the White Rabbit. He was looking everywhere, and she heard him saying, "The Duchess! The Duchess! She'll be so angry! Oh, where are they? Where did they fall?"

Alice knew that he was looking for the fan and the little gloves, and she tried to find them. But everything was changed. The hall with the little glass table and the doors had gone. She was in the country.

The White Rabbit saw her. "What are you doing out here, Mary Ann?" he asked angrily. "Run home at once and bring me some white gloves and a fan. Quick! Now!"

Alice ran towards a little house without trying to tell the White Rabbit that she was not the girl who worked for him. When she came to the door of the house, she saw "W. RABBIT" on it, and she went in. In a small room at the top of the house there was a table. Alice saw a fan and some gloves on it. She took them and went towards the door, but there was a little bottle near it. It was not like the bottle in the hall. It did not have "DRINK ME" on it, but she tried it.

"When I eat or drink anything here," she said to herself, "something always happens. Perhaps this will make me grow big again. I don't want to be small any more."

She did grow. She grew very quickly.

"Have I drunk too much?" she wondered.

She sat down. But soon she was too big for that. With her side on the floor it was better, but she was still growing. She put her arm out of the window and her foot inside the fireplace.

"I'm glad there isn't a fire," she thought. "If I grow any more, I don't know what will happen."

She stopped growing, but she could not move.

"Mary Ann! Mary Ann! Where are you? Where are my gloves?" The words came from the garden, outside the window. The Rabbit was there, and soon Alice heard his little feet as he came up to the room.

The Rabbit tried to open the door of the room, but he could not move it. Alice's back stopped it.

Alice heard him say, "Then I'll go and get in at the window."

"Oh, no, you will not!" Alice thought. She waited for the Rabbit to run round the house to the window.

There was a little cry. She heard the Rabbit calling for help, and then she heard little animals speaking.

"It's an arm."

"It's too big. It can't be an arm."

"It *is* an arm. Take it away."

Alice moved her arm. There were more cries

and a lot of noise, and then she heard the Rabbit: "We must burn the house down!"

Alice shouted, "If you do, I'll ask Dinah to catch you!" Her shout made the little house shake.

There was no answer from the little animals. She heard nothing at all for some time. Then they began to move about again.

"What will they do next?" Alice wondered.

A lot of little stones were thrown at the window. Some of them hit her arm, and some of them came through the window and hit her face and her body before they fell on the floor.

Alice looked at the stones on the floor. They all became little cakes.

"If I eat one of these cakes," she thought, "it will do something to me. It *can't* make me bigger, so it must make me smaller."

She ate one of the cakes.

At once she began to get smaller. When she was so small that she could go through the door, she ran out of the house.

There were a lot of animals outside, so Alice ran quickly until she got to some trees. It was very hard to run because she was so small. She ran round even the smallest plants and flowers.

"Oh!" Alice said, stopping and using a piece of grass as a fan. "I must grow bigger again. How can I do it? I must eat or drink something, but the question is: What?"

That *was* the question. Alice looked all round her at the flowers and the grass, but she could not see anything with "EAT ME" or "DRINK ME" on it.

There was a big mushroom growing near her. Alice went towards it. She looked under it; she looked beside it; she looked at the back of it. Then she looked to see what was on top of it.

The mushroom was as big as she was, but she could just see over the top. She looked into the eyes of a big blue caterpillar.

Chapter 5
The Caterpillar

The Caterpillar looked at Alice and said nothing.

"Perhaps it doesn't speak," Alice thought.

But at last it did speak. "Who are *you*?" it asked.

It was a hard question. Alice answered, but not very quickly: "I . . . I don't know. I knew who I was this morning, but I have changed . . . more than once . . . I think."

"How?" the Caterpillar asked.

It was another hard question. Alice said, "It's just that . . . changing from one thing to another is very hard."

"No, it isn't."

Alice thought about that. "Perhaps it isn't hard for you," she said. She knew that caterpillars change more than once before they become butterflies. "But it is hard for me."

"For *you*? Who are *you*?"

The Caterpillar had asked that question before, and Alice was near to becoming angry. She said, "Perhaps you can tell me who you are before I tell you who I am."

"Why?"

It was another hard question. Alice could not answer it, so she began to walk away.

"Come back!" the Caterpillar called. "I want

to say something."

Alice went back to the mushroom.

"You must never be angry," the Caterpillar said.

"Is that all?" Alice asked. She *was* angry.

"No."

Alice waited. "Perhaps it *will* say something if I wait," she thought.

The Caterpillar got down from the mushroom and began to move away. As it went, it said: "One side will make you grow bigger, and the other side will make you grow smaller."

Alice did not say anything, but she thought, "One side of *what*? The other side of *what*?"

Perhaps the Caterpillar heard her thinking, because it said, "Of the mushroom." Then it went into the grass, and Alice never saw it again.

Alice looked at the mushroom. It was round, like all mushrooms. "How can it have two sides – one side and the other side?" she wondered.

At last she put her arms round the top, as far as they would go. She took a bit of the mushroom with each hand.

"And now which bit will make me bigger?" she asked herself. She took a very small bite from one. "Oh!" she cried, as her head hit her foot. She just got a small bite from the other side into her mouth before it was too late. That made her bigger.

Then she tried very small bites from one side

Alice talks to the Caterpillar on the mushroom

or the other, and at last she was not too big and not too small.

"Now I must find that beautiful garden," she said.

Alice began to walk through the trees. She came to a garden, but it was not the garden that she saw before. There was a house in it – a very small house.

"I'm much too big," Alice thought. "If I go there like this, the people in the house will be afraid. I'll eat some mushroom from the part that makes me small."

Chapter 6
Pig and pepper

When Alice was not too big to go through the door, she went up to it. The house was very noisy inside.

"There's no bell," she told herself, "and nobody would hear a bell. There's too much noise."

She opened the door and went in.

She wanted to cover her ears because of the noise, but she could not do that in front of the Duchess.

The Duchess was sitting on a very small chair. She had a baby in her arms. The cook was at the fire, making soup in a very big pot.

"There's too much pepper in that soup," Alice said to herself. It was hard to say anything because the pepper made her sneeze so much. Even the Duchess was sneezing, and the baby sneezed and cried without stopping.

The cook was not sneezing, but she was making a great noise with the cooking things – CRASH! BANG! SMASH!

There was a very big cat, too, and it was not sneezing. It was sitting near the fire, and it had a grin from ear to ear on its face.

"Can girls speak first to duchesses, or must they wait for the duchesses to speak to them?" Alice wondered.

The Duchess did not speak, so Alice asked:

"Please tell me why your cat grins like that."

"It's a Cheshire cat," said the Duchess, "and that's why. *Pig!*" She shouted the last word, and Alice jumped. But the Duchess was shouting at the baby, and not at Alice, so Alice spoke again.

"I didn't know that Cheshire cats always grin. I have never seen any cat grinning."

"They all can," said the Duchess, "and most of them do."

"I didn't know that," Alice said.

"You don't know much!"

Alice thought, "I must think of something new to speak about." But just then the cook took the soup pot off the fire and began to throw things at the Duchess. One thing came through the air after another: pots, jars, irons, knives. Some of the things hit the Duchess and the baby. The Duchess did nothing, and the baby was making so much noise that it could not make any more.

"Oh, *please* don't throw any more things at the baby," Alice cried. "You'll hit its pretty nose."

"It isn't *your* baby," the Duchess said, and she began to sing to it. After every line she gave it a great shake. The words were:

Speak roughly to your little boy,
 And beat him when he sneezes:
He only does it to annoy,
 Because he knows it teases.

23

Perhaps those were not the words. It was hard for Alice to hear them because the baby was making so much noise.

"Here!" the Duchess said. "You can have the baby for a time if you like." As she was speaking, she threw the baby to Alice, adding, "I must get ready to play croquet with the Queen," and going quickly out of the room. The cook threw a pot after her, but it did not hit her.

Alice caught the baby, but it was hard to make it stay still in her arms. She took it out of the house, and after a time it stopped sneezing. It did not stop crying, but it began to make noises like a baby pig. Its eyes were becoming very small, and its nose was changing and becoming more like a pig's nose.

"It *is* a pig!" Alice told herself. She put it down on the ground, and it ran happily away, making pig noises.

Alice looked round her. She jumped a little when she saw the Cheshire Cat sitting in one of the trees near her.

The Cat only grinned when it saw Alice.

"It looks kind," she thought, "but perhaps it will get angry quickly like all the people and animals here." So she tried to speak in a pleasing way.

"Cheshire Cat, dear," she said.

Its grin grew bigger, not smaller, so she knew that it was pleased.

Alice sees the Cheshire Cat sitting in a tree

"Will you tell me, please," she said, "which way I must go from here?"

"Yes," said the Cat, "but mustn't you tell me where you want to go?"

"Well, any place——" Alice began.

"Then you can go any way," the Cat said.

"——if it *is* a place," Alice said.

"If you walk *that* way, you'll get to a Hatter's house. Hatters make hats, you know. And if you walk *that* way, you'll find a March Hare. The Hatter's mad, and the March Hare's mad."

"But I don't want to meet mad people," Alice said.

"Oh, there's no way *not* to meet them. We're all mad here. I'm mad. You're mad."

"How do you know I'm mad?" Alice asked.

"You must be mad," the Cat said. "Everybody who comes here is mad. Are you going to play croquet with the Queen today?"

"That would be very nice," said Alice, "but nobody has asked me yet."

"You'll see me there," the Cheshire Cat said.

It did not go away, but it was not there any more. It just disappeared. Alice did not wonder about this, but she was still looking at the place when it appeared again. "What happened to the baby?" it asked.

"It became a pig," Alice said.

"I thought it would," said the Cat, and disappeared again.

Alice waited. "Perhaps it will appear again," she thought. But it did not appear, and she began to walk towards the March Hare's home.

"I have seen hatters before," she said to herself. "I would like to see a March Hare. This is May, not March, so perhaps the March Hare isn't *very* mad."

Just then, she looked up, and there was the Cheshire Cat again, sitting in another tree.

"Did you say pig, or fig?" said the Cat.

"I said pig," Alice answered. "And please stop appearing and disappearing so quickly. I don't like it."

The Cat disappeared a little at a time. The last part that Alice could see was its grin. It was there after the other parts had gone.

"I have seen a cat without a grin very many times," Alice thought, "but a grin without a cat! I never saw anything like that before."

When the Cheshire Cat's grin had gone, Alice began to walk again towards the March Hare's house. She saw it through the trees, and it was not so small as the Duchess's house. Alice had the bits of mushroom in her pockets. She quickly ate a little of the bit that made her bigger. Then she walked towards the house.

Chapter 7
At the tea table

There was a tree in front of the house. A big table under the tree had places for a lot of people, but there were only three at it: the Hatter, the March Hare, and a dormouse. The Dormouse was asleep, and the other two were sitting very near to it, one on each side, and speaking over its head.

When they saw Alice, the Hatter and the March Hare cried out, "No, no! There isn't a place for you!"

"There are a lot of places," Alice said, and she sat down in a big chair.

The Hatter looked at her and took a watch out of his pocket. "What day is it?" he asked.

Alice thought. Then she said, "Wednesday, I think."

"It's Friday by my watch," the Hatter said to the March Hare, looking unhappy. "I told you that butter wasn't good for a watch."

"It was the best butter," the March Hare said.

"Yes, but you put it in with the bread knife. Some bread got in, perhaps."

The March Hare took the watch and looked at it sadly. Then he put it in his tea; took it out; looked at it sadly again; and said again, "It was the best butter."

Alice sits down at the March Hare's tea table

Alice looked at the watch. "It tells the day," she said, "but it doesn't tell you the time of day."

"Why should it?" the Hatter asked. "Does *your* watch tell you what year it is?"

"No," Alice answered, "but that's because it's the same year for a very long time."

"And *my* watch doesn't tell the time because it's always tea time."

Alice wondered about that, but she said nothing.

"Take some more tea," the March Hare said to her.

Alice said, "Thank you. But I haven't had any yet, so I can't take more."

"Yes, you can," the Hatter said. "Anybody can take more than nothing."

Alice did not like the way the Hatter spoke to her. "I don't think he should speak to me like that," she thought. And she began to tell him: "I don't think——"

"Then you shouldn't speak," the Hatter said.

Alice was angry. She walked away from the table. "Perhaps they'll call me back," she thought. "And then they'll be nice to me and give me some tea and bread-and-butter."

But they did not say anything. She looked back once. The Dormouse was still asleep, and the Hatter and the March Hare were trying to put it into the teapot.

"I'll never go *there* again," Alice said. And

she tried to tell herself, "I didn't *want* any tea or bread-and-butter."

Just as she said that, she saw a door in one of the trees.

"I have never seen a door in a tree before," she thought. "I wonder where it goes." And she went in.

She found herself in the long hall, near the little glass table.

"I'll get through the little door into the garden this time," she said to herself. She took the little golden key and opened the little door. Then she took very small bites from the bit of mushroom that made her smaller. When she was not too big and not too small, she walked through the door. At last she was in the beautiful garden.

Chapter 8
Croquet with the Queen

The prettiest flowers in the garden were the roses. There were some on a small tree. Alice stopped to look at them. They were white roses, but three gardeners were working hard, trying to make them red.

"Why are they doing that?" Alice wondered. She went near them.

"Please can you tell me," she asked, "why you are making those roses red?"

The three gardeners looked very unhappy.

"You tell her, Seven," one of them said.

"No," said Seven, "you tell her, Five."

But Five said, "No, you tell her, Two."

Two looked even more unhappy, but he began, "Well, Miss, this ... er ... this ... er ... tree should be a red rose tree. If the Queen sees white roses on it, she'll ... er ... she'll have our heads cut off. So we're trying to make them red before she comes to ... er ... "

Five was looking across the garden, and just then he cried out, "The Queen! The Queen!"

At once the three gardeners threw themselves down with their faces on the ground.

Alice heard a great noise. "Now I shall see the Queen!" she thought.

It was a procession. Ten soldiers came in front of

The gardeners try to make the roses red

all the others. They were like the gardeners, but they had clubs like this ♣ . Then Alice saw ten of the King's own men with red diamonds ♦ on them. The children of the King and Queen came next, all with red hearts ♥ . After them there were the people who had come to play croquet. Most of them were kings and queens, but Alice saw that one of them was the White Rabbit, not looking at all happy. The Knave of Hearts came next, just in front of the King and Queen of Hearts themselves.

"Should I lie on my face like the gardeners?" Alice wondered. "But what is a procession for, if nobody looks at it?" So she stood and waited.

When the procession came to Alice, they all stopped and looked at her. The Queen said to the Knave of Hearts, "Who is this?"

The Knave of Hearts did not know, so he said nothing.

"Fool!" the Queen shouted. Then she spoke to Alice. "What's your name, child?"

"My name is Alice, if you please." And Alice wondered if that was the way to speak to a queen. "But they're only a pack of cards," she told herself. "I'm not going to be afraid of them."

The Queen looked at the three gardeners who were on their faces round the rose tree. She could not see who they were because their backs were the same as the backs of all the others: the

The Queen of Hearts asks Alice who she is

same as three soldiers; or three of the King's own men; or even three of her own children.

"Who are these?" the Queen asked.

"Don't ask *me*! Why should I know?" said Alice. "That was very brave of me," she thought.

The Queen's face became very red. She was very, very angry. She looked at Alice and shouted: "Off with her head! Off——"

"Nonsense!" said Alice.

The Queen did not know what to do. The King put his hand on his wife's arm and said, "Don't be angry, my dear. She's only a child."

She moved her arm away angrily. "Show me their faces," she said to the Knave.

The Knave moved the gardeners with his foot.

"Get up!" the Queen shouted, and they stood up, very much afraid, and saying nothing.

"*What*," the Queen asked, "have you been doing?"

"If you please," began Two, "we ... er ... we were trying——"

"I *see*!" said the Queen. She had been looking at the roses. "Off with their heads!"

The procession moved on, but three soldiers stayed to cut the gardeners' heads off. The gardeners ran to Alice for help, and she put them into a big flower pot. "Don't be afraid," she said. "They will not cut your heads off."

The soldiers looked round the garden for some time. Then they went after the procession.

"Are their heads off?" the Queen shouted.

"Their heads have gone, if you please," they shouted back.

"Good!" shouted the Queen. "Can you play croquet?"

The soldiers said nothing, but they looked at Alice. The question was for her.

"Yes," Alice called out.

"Come on, then!" the Queen cried, and Alice went and took her place in the procession.

"What will happen next?" she wondered.

"It's ... it's a nice day, isn't it?" she heard.

The White Rabbit was beside her. He was looking at her face to see if she was angry with him.

"Yes, a very nice day," Alice said. "Where's the Duchess?"

"Sh!" The Rabbit looked all round him quickly.

Then he put his mouth near to Alice's ear and said: "She's going to have her head cut off."

"Is she? Why?" Alice said.

"Did you say, 'I shall cry'?" the Rabbit asked.

"No, I didn't. I shall not cry. I said, 'Why?'"

"She hit the Queen," the Rabbit began.

"Oh, good!" Alice said.

"Sh!" the Rabbit said again. (Alice could see that he was afraid.) "The Queen will hear you. She hears everything. The Duchess came late, and the Queen said——"

"Go to your places!" shouted the Queen, and people began to run about everywhere. They ran into other people and fell down. Alice could see that they were all afraid of the Queen. But after a time they were ready, and the game began.

This croquet was not the game Alice knew. At home people hit a ball with a wooden "mallet" to send it over the grass. Here somebody gave her a flamingo to hit a hedgehog. Some of the ground was grassy, and some was not.

When her flamingo was ready to hit the hedgehog, the hedgehog walked away. When the hedgehog was a ball again, the flamingo put its head up and looked at her. "It's a very hard game," Alice thought.

The game was hard for everybody, and the Queen was becoming angrier and angrier. She went round shouting "Off with his head!" or "Off with her head!"

Alice didn't *see* any heads being cut off, but she was not happy. "The Queen isn't angry with me just now," she thought, "but it can happen at any time. I *would* like to speak to somebody about it."

There was something in the air near her. "I wonder what it is," she said. And then she saw that it was a grin. "It's the Cheshire Cat," she thought. "Now I shall have somebody to speak to."

As soon as its mouth was all there, the Cheshire Cat said, "How are you? Are you happy?"

Alice waited. When she could see its eyes, she shook her head. "I can't speak to it," she thought, "before it has some ears – or perhaps one ear."

Soon she could see its head, with the ears, and Alice said, "I don't like the game at all. It isn't a good game."

The Cat did not show any more of itself. Its head stayed in the air without a body. "How do you like the Queen?" it asked.

"I don't," said Alice. She saw that the Queen was very near, and she added "... think ... I don't think that there is any queen like her."

The Queen was pleased, and moved away. But the King came to Alice and stood by her, looking at the Cat's head and wondering. "Who *are* you speaking to?" he asked Alice.

"It's a friend of mine," Alice said, "a Cheshire cat."

"I don't like the look of it at all," said the King, "but it may kiss my hand, if it likes."

"I don't want to," the Cat said.

The King was angry, but he was afraid too. "Don't look at me like that," he said to the Cat, and he stood on the other side of Alice.

Alice said, "A cat may look at a king. I read that in a book, I think."

"Well, it must go," the King said, and he called to the Queen. "This cat must go, my dear, mustn't it?"

The Queen did not even look. "Off with his head!" she shouted.

"I'll get the axeman myself," the King said, and he went away quickly.

Just then, Alice lost her flamingo. It tried to fly up into a tree, and she could not catch it for some time.

When Alice got back to the Cheshire Cat, there were a lot of people round it. The King and the Queen and the axeman were all speaking at the same time.

The axeman was saying: "I can't cut a head off if there isn't a body to cut it off."

The King was saying: "Nonsense! If anything has a head, its head can be cut off."

The Queen was saying: "If somebody doesn't do something soon, I'll have *everybody's* head cut off."

As soon as Alice came, they all asked her about it. Alice thought, and then she said, "It's the Duchess's cat. Ask *her* about it."

"Bring the Duchess here," the Queen said. "She's waiting to have her head cut off."

The axeman ran to get the Duchess, and the Cheshire Cat's head began to disappear. Even its grin had disappeared by the time the Duchess came. The King and the axeman ran about, trying to find it, but the Queen told all the others to go back to the game.

"Come for a walk," the Duchess said, and she put her arm through Alice's arm. "I'm very glad to see you again." And they walked away.

Alice heard the Queen at the croquet ground. She was still shouting "Off with his head!" and "Off with her head!" as she got angry with the players.

"You must be glad to be alive," Alice said to the Duchess.

"Yes," the Duchess said. "It's a nice day."

"Will they still cut your head off?"

"Oh, no! They never cut anybody's head off. The Queen likes to say it, but nobody does it."

Alice wanted to ask some more questions, but they heard a cry of "The trial's beginning!"

"What trial is it?" Alice tried to ask, but the Duchess was running too quickly to answer. As she still had Alice's arm, Alice ran too.

Alice and the Duchess go for a walk

Chapter 9
Who stole the tarts?

The King and Queen of Hearts were sitting down, and the trial was ready to begin when Alice went into the courtroom. Alice had never been in a courtroom, but she had seen pictures of courts, and she knew something about them from books.

The Knave of Hearts was standing in front of the King and Queen. His head was down, and there was a soldier on each side of him. It was his trial.

Alice found a place, and then she looked round her. She saw a lot of the animals and birds that she knew. And there were some tarts on a table in the court. They looked very good.

When everybody was ready, the King called out: "Read the paper!"

The White Rabbit stood up. From a very big paper he read out:

"The Queen of Hearts, she made some tarts,
All on a summer day.
The Knave of Hearts, he stole those tarts,
And took them all away."

"Off with his head!" cried the Queen.

Alice could see that the White Rabbit was

43

afraid, but he said, "Not yet, not yet! We must have witnesses."

"Call a witness," said the King.

The Hatter came into the court as a witness. He had his tea in one hand and some bread-and-butter in the other hand.

"I was having my tea when they called me," he said.

"Why?" asked the King. "When did you begin your tea?"

The Hatter thought. He looked at the March Hare and the Dormouse, who had come into court with him. Then he said, "March the fourteenth, I think."

"Fifteenth," said the March Hare.

"Sixteenth," added the Dormouse.

"Write that down," said the King. Then he said to the Hatter, "Take off your hat."

"It isn't mine," said the Hatter.

"You stole it?" The King looked angry.

The Hatter was so afraid that he began to shake.

"No, no! I *sell* them. I'm a poor man. I haven't any hats of my own. I'm a hatter!"

"Don't be afraid," the King said, "or I'll tell them to cut your head off. What did you see?"

"I'm a poor man," the Hatter said, still shaking. "I was having my tea when the March Hare said——"

"I didn't!" the March Hare cried quickly.

The White Rabbit with the very big paper

"Well, the Dormouse said ... " The Hatter waited for the Dormouse to say "I didn't" but the Dormouse was asleep.

"After that," the Hatter said, "I cut some more bread-and-butter."

"But what did the Dormouse say?"

"I can't remember," the Hatter said.

"You *must* remember," the King said, "or I'll have your head cut off."

The unhappy Hatter was shaking more and more "I'm a poor man ... " he began.

The King wanted to hear the next witness. "You may go," he said to the Hatter.

The Hatter ran out of the court as the Queen said, "And cut his head off outside!" But he was running so quickly that the axeman could not catch him.

Alice was wondering why the courtroom was becoming smaller. She thought about it. "Perhaps I am growing bigger," she told herself.

"Call the next witness," said the King.

Alice did not know who the next witness was. But people at the door began to sneeze, and then everybody in the court sneezed, as the Duchess's cook came in with her pepper pot.

The King looked at her. "Are you the next witness?" he asked.

There was no answer.

"Tell us everything that you know," said the King.

Who stole the tarts?

The trial

47

"No!" said the cook.

"You must ask her some questions," the White Rabbit told the King.

"Oh!" the King said. He thought hard, and then he asked, "What are tarts made of?"

"Pepper, mostly," the cook said, and she shook her pepper pot.

When everybody had stopped sneezing, they looked for the cook, but she had disappeared.

"Call the next witness," said the King.

Alice wondered who the next witness would be. "The witnesses haven't said anything yet," she thought.

The White Rabbit looked at his paper. He read out the next name: "Alice!"

Chapter 10
The end of the trial

"Here!" cried Alice, and she stood up.

She did not remember that she had been growing. When she stood up, the chairs and tables and other things and the people in the courtroom fell about – here, there, and everywhere.

Alice put them back in their places. Then she looked at the King. He was writing something. He looked at Alice and then read: "Rule Forty-two: No person as big as a house may stay in the court."

"I'm not as big as a house ... " Alice began.

"You are," said the King.

"Nearly twice as big," the Queen added. She was very angry.

" ... and it's not a rule," Alice said. "You have just written it."

"It's the oldest rule of all," the King told her.

"Then," said Alice, "it should be Rule One, not Rule Forty-two." She was not afraid of them because she had grown so big.

"Off with her head!" shouted the Queen.

"Nonsense!" said Alice. "Who's afraid of you? You're only a pack of cards!"

The pack of cards – all fifty-two of them – went up into the air and came down on top of

All the cards go up in the air

her. Alice began to fight them, partly afraid, and partly angry. She opened her eyes, and ...

She was on the grass; some leaves had fallen from the tree on to her, and her sister was moving them off her face.

"Wake up, Alice dear!" her sister said. "What a long sleep you have had!"

Questions

Questions on each chapter

1 *Down the rabbit hole*
   1 Where were Alice and her sister? (They were . . .)
   2 Where did the White Rabbit go? (Down . . .)
   3 What was Dinah?
   4 Where was the key? (On . . .)
   5 What was on the other side of the door?

2 *The pool of tears*
   1 What did the cake do to Alice? (It made her . . .)
   2 Why couldn't she go through the door?
     (Because she was too . . .)
   3 What was making Alice smaller?
   4 What was the water? (It was a pool of . . .)
   5 What animal was in the water?

3 *A Caucus race*
   1 Who asked the Dodo a question?
   2 Who gave the prizes to the birds and animals?
   3 What were the prizes?
   4 What was the prize for Alice?
   5 Who gave Alice her prize?

4 *The White Rabbit's house*
   1 What was the White Rabbit looking for?
     (His . . . and his . . .)
   2 Where was the bottle?
   3 The Rabbit couldn't open the door. Why?
   4 What did the stones become?
   5 What was on top of the mushroom?

5 *The Caterpillar*
   1 What do caterpillars become?

2 What question did the Caterpillar ask twice?
3 "One side of *what*?" What was the answer?
4 How many bits of mushroom did Alice take?
5 What was in the garden?

6 *Pig and pepper*
  1 Where was the baby when Alice went in?
  2 Who threw things at the Duchess?
  3 Where did Alice take the baby?
  4 What did the baby become?
  5 Which part of the Cheshire Cat disappeared last?

7 *At the tea table*
  1 Who said, "There isn't a place for you"?
  2 Where did the March Hare put the watch?
  3 Where was the door?
  4 What was on the other side of the door?
  5 How did Alice make herself smaller? (She took . . .)

8 *Croquet with the Queen*
  1 What were the gardeners trying to do to the roses?
  2 What were the names of the three gardeners?
  3 What question did the Queen ask Alice?
  4 Why did three soldiers stay there? (To . . .)
  5 Why is the Duchess not in the procession?
  6 Who went to get the axeman?
  7 Whose cat was it?

9 *Who stole the tarts?*
  1 What room were the King and Queen in?
  2 Who made the tarts?
  3 Who came into the court with the Hatter?
  4 What made everybody sneeze?
  5 What was the next name on the list of witnesses?

10 *The end of the trial*
  1 Why did everything and everybody fall about?
  2 What was "Rule Forty-two"?
  3 Why was Alice not afraid? (Because . . .)
  4 What were the Queen's last words?
  5 When Alice opened her eyes, where was she?

Questions on the whole story

These are harder questions. Read the Introduction, and think hard about the questions before you answer them. Some of them ask for your opinion, and there is no fixed answer.

1 Most of the story is Alice's dream. She is asleep. Can you find
   a the words that start her dream?
   b the words which show that her dream has ended?

2 a How old do you think Alice is?
   b Try to say why you think that is her age.

3 Here are some English sayings. Can you find places in the story that could make readers think of the sayings?
   a "as dead as a dodo"
   b "to grin like a Cheshire cat"
   c "as mad as a hatter"
   d "as mad as a March hare"
   e "A cat may look at a king."

4 Find these words and answer the questions.
   a "How angry she'll be because I'm late!"
      1 Who said it? 2 What was he wearing?
      3 Who heard him?
   b "I don't want to be my friend Mabel."
      1 Who said it? 2 Where was the speaker?
      3 What reason did she give for not wanting to be Mabel?
   c "Please take this very beautiful box with our thanks."
      1 Who said it? 2 Whose box was it?
      3 Why was it "our" thanks? 4 What were the thanks for?

5 People and creatures are often angry in this story. Can you say what made them angry in these parts of the story?
   a The Mouse in the pool of tears
   b Alice at the mushroom
   c The cook in the Duchess's kitchen
   d Alice at the Mad Hatter's tea table
   e The Queen in the rose garden

6 Is there a person or creature in this story that you like better than the others? Can you give reasons?

7 Is there a person or creature you do not like? If so, why not?

New words

annoy
: make (somebody) angry

bat
: a small flying animal (not a bird)

butterfly
: a beautiful flying insect

caterpillar
: a leaf-eating creature that goes on many legs. It becomes a butterfly.

croquet
: a game played on grass. You try to make a wooden ball go through a bent iron "hoop".

dormouse
: a small forest animal. It sleeps in the winter.

flamingo
: a big white and red bird with a long neck and very long legs

grin
: (have) a very wide smile

hedgehog
: a small animal. It rolls into a prickly ball when it is afraid.

mad
: with a disordered mind

mouse
: a very small animal. Plural: mice

mushroom
: a low white plant, without leaves, that you can eat

nonsense
: words that mean nothing

pack of cards
: a set of 52 cards of four kinds (clubs ♣, diamonds ♦, hearts ♥, spades ♠) used in games.

pepper
: hot-tasting powder used in cooking

pig
: a farm animal that is eaten in some countries

pool
: a place where a small amount of water has collected

prize
: something that we give to the winner of a race, etc

procession
a line of people going
somewhere in a fixed order

soup
hot liquid food made by
boiling meat, etc, in water

tart
a round piece of pastry with
fruit in it

tease
make (somebody) angry

trial
a judge's court hearing of a
law case

witness
a person who has seen a
happening and tells about it
in a **trial**